ISBN 0-590-61729-X

12 11 10 9 8 7 6 5   0/0

Printed in the U.S.A.   08

First Scholastic printing, October 1995

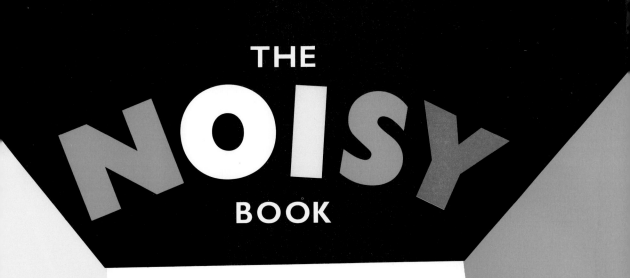

THE NOISY BOOK

by Margaret Wise Brown

pictures by Leonard Weisgard

Scholastic Inc.
New York Toronto London Auckland Sydney

One day a little dog named Muffin got a cinder in his eye. Poor little Muffin. His eye hurt him. It stung. So they took him to the dog doctor.

The dog doctor said, "Muffin, I will put this bandage over your eyes and when you take it off tonight your eye won't hurt you any more."

And there was Muffin with a great big white bandage over his eyes.

**Everything looked as dark to him
as when you close your eyes**

BUT

MUFFIN COULD HEAR

Muffin pricked up his ears

**he heard everything in the
room that made a noise**

he heard

TICK TOCK TICK TOCK

(it was the clock)

he heard

SISSS SISSSSSSS

(it was the radiator)

he heard

SNIP SNAP SNIP SNAP

(it was a pair of scissors)

he heard

TING A LING A LING

(it was the telephone)

he heard

GRRRRRR GRRRRRRR

(it was his own stomach growling)

he heard

BZZZ BZZZzzzzzzz

(it was a little black fly)

he heard

KERCHOOO

(it was the dog doctor sneezing)

Then Muffin went down the
street on his way home.
"Poor little Muffin," said the
people on the street.
"Muffin has a big white bandage
over his eyes and he can't
see a thing."

But
Muffin could hear.

Muffin pricked up his
ears and heard all the
noises on the street.

First he heard the big noises

MEN HAMMERING
Bang bang bang

AUTOMOBILE HORNS
Awuurra awuurra

HORSES' HOOFS
Clop clop Clop clop

ANOTHER LITTLE DOG
Bow wow wow

Then he heard the biggest noise on the street

**Then the sun began to shine
Could Muffin hear that?**

Then he heard the little noises

Bzzzzzz bzzzzzz
a bee
Swishhhh swishhh
car wheels
Chirp chirp
a bird
Meoww meoww
a pussycat
Patter patter patter patter
people's feet
Flippity flap flap flap
an awning in the wind

It began to snow
But could Muffin hear that?

Then he heard a little noise

and he didn't know what it was

squeak

squeak

squeak

It was not a mouse

What could it be?

Was it

a big horse going squeak squeak squeak?

NO

Was it

a policeman going squeak squeak squeak?

NO

Was it

a garbage can?

NO

Was it

a big fierce lion?

NO

Was it

an empty house?

NO

Was it

an engine and a coal car?

NO

Was it

a big boat?

NO

Was it

an airplane?

NO

What do Y O U think it was?

It was a BABY DOLL

**And they gave the baby doll
to Muffin for his very own.**